BEWARE
OF BOYS

Tony Blundell

PUFFIN BOOKS

To the wolf, without whom . . .

PUFFIN BOOKS

Published by the Penguin Group
Penguin Books Ltd, 80 Strand, London WC2R 0RL, England
Penguin Group (USA), Inc., 375 Hudson Street, New York, New York 10014, USA
Penguin Books Australia Ltd, 250 Camberwell Road, Camberwell, Victoria 3124, Australia
Penguin Books Canada Ltd, 10 Alcorn Avenue, Toronto, Ontario, Canada M4V 3B2
Penguin Books India (P) Ltd, 11 Community Centre, Panchsheel Park, New Delhi – 110 017, India
Penguin Group (NZ), cnr Airborne and Rosedale Roads, Albany, Auckland 1310, New Zealand
Penguin Books (South Africa) (Pty) Ltd, 24 Sturdee Avenue, Rosebank 2196, South Africa

Penguin Books Ltd, Registered Offices: 80 Strand, London WC2R 0RL, England

www.penguin.com

First published by Viking 1991
Published in Picture Puffins in 1993
17 19 20 18

Copyright © Tony Blundell, 1991
All rights reserved

The moral right of the author/illustrator has been asserted

Set in Sabon 17/22pt

Manufactured in China

British Library Cataloguing in Publication Data
A CIP catalogue record for this book is available from the British Library

ISBN-13: 978-0-14054-156-4

Once upon a time, not so very long ago, nor so very far away, a small boy took a short cut through the forest ...

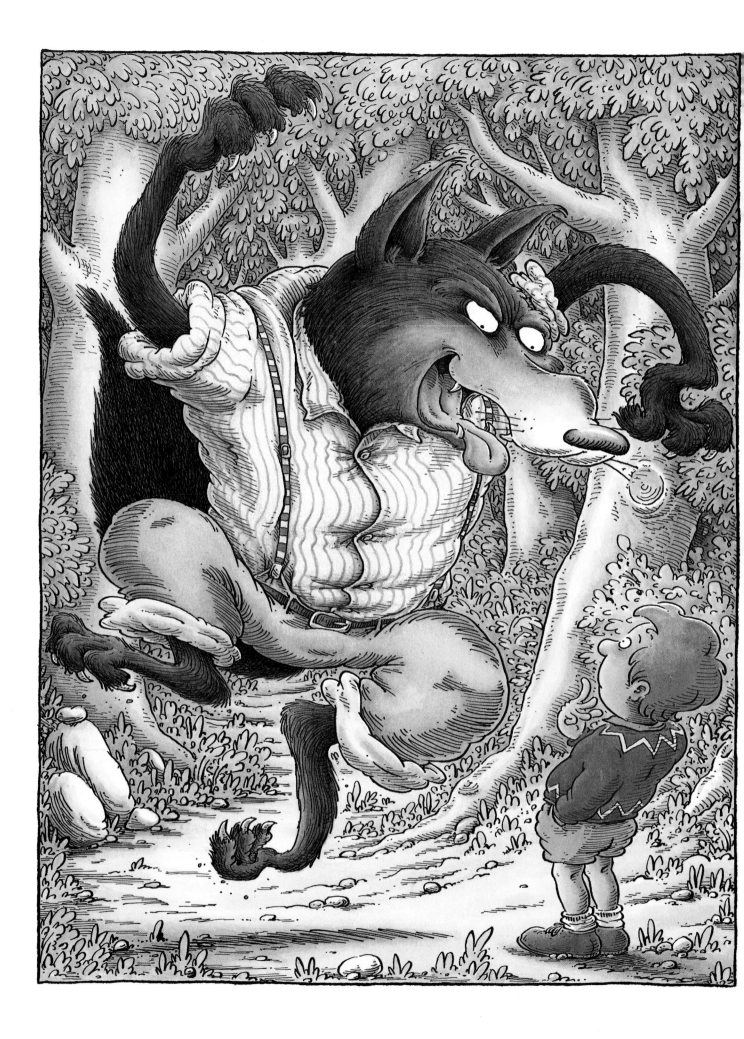

... and was captured by a hungry wolf.

"Silly boy," smiled the wolf, and carried him back to his cave.

"What are you going to do with me?" asked the boy.
The wolf licked his lips. "Why, eat you, of course," he replied.

"Raw?" said the boy.
The wolf roared.
"No," sighed the boy, "I mean, aren't you even going to cook me first?"
The wolf thought about it.

"Go on, then," he said. "What do you suggest?"

"I do just happen to know a very good recipe for Boy Soup."
The wolf, who was both hungry and greedy, could hardly
contain himself.
"MMMMMMMMMM!" he dribbled. "Tell me what I need."
So the boy told him.

Recipe for Boy Soup

Ingredients:

(to serve one greedy wolf)

One boy (medium-sized)

One large iron pot

One tonne of potatoes

One oodle of onions

One wooden tub of turnips

One cartload of carrots

One packet of fruity chews

One wellful of water

One barrel of bricks

One trowel

Method:

1. First catch your boy.

2. Wash him thoroughly, especially behind the ears.

3. Place him firmly in the iron pot.

4. Add water, potatoes, onions, turnips, carrots and fruity chews to taste.

5. Sit on the barrel of bricks and stir with the trowel until Thursday.

Off the wolf ran to gather the ingredients.
He raced here and there

to and fro

up and down

round and round

over and under

this way and that.

When the wolf returned, the boy checked through everything. "Oh, silly wolf," he said. "You have forgotten the salt!"

The wolf's face fell.
"But you didn't say salt!" he spluttered.
"Well, not to worry," said the boy. "I've just remembered an even more delicious dish which, as it happens, needs no salt!"

The wolf's stomach started to rumble rather badly.
"Great stuff!" he said. "Tell me, tell me!"

"It's called Boy Pie," said the boy, popping a fruity chew
into his mouth, "and it's three times as good as Boy Soup!"

"Yummmm!" said the wolf.
"... but you will just need a few things ... "

Recipe for Boy Pie

Ingredients:

(to serve one greedy and
bad-tempered wolf)

One boy (not too skinny)

One large pie dish

Three foothills of plain flour

One moo-cow of milk

One large lump of lard

Six sacks of cement

One load of leeks

One bird bath of beans

One packing case of parsnips

One shovel

One cowboy hat

One yellow yo-yo

Method:

1. Toss the flour, milk and lard with the shovel until done.
2. Arrange the boy comfortably in the pie dish.
3. Fill his pockets with vegetables and cover with pastry.
4. Place the yo-yo in the hat and sit on it.
5. Inspect the pie hourly, then daily, until golden brown.

Off scampered the wolf.
He scurried here and there

to and fro

up and down

round and round

over and under

this way and that.

When the wolf came struggling back, huffing and puffing, the boy examined the goods.

"Oh, wolf," he said, "silly wolf, you have forgotten the salt!" The wolf went weak at the knees.

"But you said this one needed no salt!" he groaned. "Well, it does," said the boy, "but never mind. I've just remembered the most fantastically scrumptious dish that ever was – and it definitely doesn't need salt!"

The wolf had almost decided on raw boy again.

He pricked up his ears.

"Go on, then," he growled. "Tell me!"

"It's called Boy Cake," said the boy, "and it's ten times better than Boy Pie!"

"And I suppose . . . " sighed the wolf hopelessly, " . . . that I will just need a few things?"

"Right!" said the boy.

Recipe for Boy Cake

Ingredients:

(to serve one ravenously hungry and exhausted wolf)

One boy (as fat as you like)

One bathtub

One big blob of butter

One binful of brown sugar

Five fire buckets of self-raising flour

One handbag of hens' eggs

One brick outhouse

One wheelbarrow of walnuts

One carrier bag of currants

One bunch of bananas

One red bicycle

Two barn doors

One seashore of sand

One bunch of daffodils

Method:

1. Place the boy in a warm room and allow to watch television.
2. Mix the butter, flour, brown sugar and hens' eggs in the bathtub.
3. Blend in the barn doors, bananas, currants and walnuts.
4. Carefully add the bicycle, sand and daffodils.
5. If it rains, stand in the outhouse.

The wolf crawled off once more into the forest.
He stumbled here and there

to and fro

up and down

round and round

over and under

this way and that.

It was some time before the wolf returned, staggering under
an enormous mountain of ingredients.
The boy took a long, long look.

"Oh, silly, silly wolf!" he said, shaking his head sadly.
"You have forgotten the salt."

There was a tremendous crash as the wolf collapsed.

Down went the wolf.

Down came the barn doors.

Down came the bicycle.

Down came the outhouse.

Down came the wheelbarrow, the walnuts and the currants.

Down came the fire buckets, the butter and the bin.

Down came the bananas, the hens' eggs and the sand.

Luckily, the boy managed to catch the daffodils.

The wolf lay stunned.
"Napping in the afternoon, wolf, tut-tut," said the boy, as he mixed together the cement,
the water and the sand.

"You really should take a little more exercise," he said, as he placed brick upon brick, and built a wall right across the mouth of the wolf's cave.

"Silly old wolf," he thought, as he rode the red bicycle back through the forest.

When he got home, his mother was waiting for him.

"Mother, Mother," he cried, "I took a short cut through the forest, and was captured by a hungry wolf, and he gave me these sweets, and this hat, and a new bike ... and he sent you these flowers!"

"He sounds like a nice chap," said his mother. "Now sit down and eat up your supper while it's hot."

Which is more than the wolf did that night!

MORAL OF THIS STORY: Never forget the salt!